Jane Eyre

CHARLOTTE BRONTË

Level 3

Retold by Ann Ward
Series Editors: Andy Hopkins and Jocelyn Potter

Pearson Education Limited

Edinburgh Gate, Harlow,
Essex CM20 2JE, England
and Associated Companies throughout the world.

ISBN: 978-1-4058-7663-6

Jane Eyre was first published in 1847
This adaptation first published by Penguin Books Ltd 1991
Published by Addison Wesley Longman Ltd and Penguin Books Ltd 1998
New edition first published 1999
This edition first published 2008

3 5 7 9 10 8 6 4 2

Text copyright © Ann Ward 1991
Illustrations copyright © Richard Johnson 1991

The moral right of the adapter and of the illustrator has been asserted

Typeset by Graphicraft Ltd, Hong Kong
Set in 11/14pt Bembo
Printed in China
SWTC/02

Published by Pearson Education Ltd in association with
Penguin Books Ltd, both companies being subsidiaries of Pearson Plc

For a complete list of the titles available in the Penguin Readers series please write to your local
Pearson Longman office or to: Penguin Readers Marketing Department, Pearson Education,
Edinburgh Gate, Harlow, Essex CM20 2JE, England.

Contents

Introduction

Someone was in my room. It was a woman. She was a big woman, tall and strong. At first I did not see her face. She looked at herself in the mirror. Then I saw her face! It was the most terrible face. She looked angry, cruel and frightening.

Jane Eyre has no mother or father. She lives with a cruel aunt and three cousins. Her life changes when her aunt sends her away to live at Lowood School. Jane is happier there, but Mr Brocklehurst, the owner of the school, is unkind and mean with his money. The girls do not have enough warm clothes or food. Jane stays there until she is eighteen years old. Then she finds a teaching job and goes to work for Mr Rochester. He owns a large house, Thornfield Hall, and there Jane teaches a little French girl, Adèle. But after a time, Jane falls in love with Mr Rochester. Does Mr Rochester love her? Is Jane right to love him? Or is he going to marry the rich Blanche Ingram?

Mr Rochester is very rich, and Jane is poor. But more important than that, Thornfield Hall holds a terrible secret. Why does Grace Poole, a servant, live in the attic? Who walks around the house at night and laughs strangely outside Jane's bedroom door? Why does Mr Mason come from the West Indies to visit Mr Rochester? And why is Mr Rochester afraid of Mason? Only Mr Rochester knows the answers – and he will say nothing . . .

Charlotte Brontë was born in 1816 in a village in Yorkshire, in the north of England. The family soon moved to a village called Haworth. Her father was the village clergyman, and their house was next to the church. Her mother died when Charlotte was five years old. An aunt came to look after the six children. In 1824, the four oldest sisters, Maria, Elizabeth, Charlotte and Emily, went away to school. The school was a cold, unhappy place, and the girls did not have enough to eat. Maria and Elizabeth became ill and died. This is the school that Charlotte later describes as Lowood in *Jane Eyre*. After that, Charlotte, her two younger sisters and her brother Branwell had their lessons at home. They began to write stories together. They called their stories *The Gondal Chronicles*. Some of these writings still exist. Charlotte was now the oldest. She spent three years away from home teaching in a school, and then she lived with two local families as a teacher to their children.

In 1842 Charlotte and Emily went to Belgium to study French in Brussels. There Charlotte fell in love with the husband of the owner of the language school where she was studying. But there was no hope for Charlotte: lonely and unhappy, she returned home.

The three sisters, Charlotte, Emily and Anne, continued to write. In 1846, they decided to bring out a book of poems, using the names Currer, Ellis and Acton Bell. They found a book company to take their work, but it sold very few copies of the *Poems*. The sisters then each tried to sell stories to the book company. Anne sent *Agnes Grey* and Emily sent *Wuthering Heights*. Both books came out in 1847. Charlotte sent *The Professor*, a story about a young woman and a Belgian teacher, but the company did not like it. She then sent *Jane Eyre*, and this story came out that same year, 1847. It was an immediate success. Suddenly, everybody wanted to meet Currer, Ellis and Acton Bell. Charlotte was now famous, but terrible unhappiness followed. Her brother and sisters all died: Branwell in September 1848, Emily in December of the same year and Anne the next March.

Charlotte continued to write. *Shirley* (1849) is a story that happens in Yorkshire. It is about the lives of men and women factory workers and their cruel employers. *Villette* (1853) happens in Belgium and is similar to *The Professor* but a much better story. *The Professor*, her first book, came out after Charlotte's death, and many people find it the weakest of her works.

Charlotte received many offers of marriage. She finally chose a young clergyman, her father's assistant. They married in 1854 but Charlotte died in March of the next year. After her death, her father, Patrick Brontë, asked Mrs Gaskell, another well-known writer, to write the story of Charlotte's life. This book, *The Life of Charlotte Brontë* (1857), made her even more famous.

Jane Eyre is Charlotte Brontë's best known book. Jane is a good and kind person with a strong sense of right and wrong. She also has deep feelings. The many difficulties that she has do not shake her love for the mysterious Mr Rochester. But when she discovers his secret, she has to leave Thornfield Hall. Another man, St John Rivers, comes into her life, but she does not love him. He wants to marry Jane and take her with him to India. But Jane's love for Mr Rochester has not died. *Jane Eyre* is one of the world's greatest love stories.

It was first made into a film – a silent film – in 1910, and again in 1914 and 1921. The first film of *Jane Eyre* with sound was in 1934. In 1944 another film of this story was made with Orson Welles playing Mr Rochester and Joan Fontaine as Jane. In 1996, Franco Zeffirelli made another film with William Hurt and Charlotte Gainsbourg. Every five or ten years, there is a made-for-TV film of *Jane Eyre*. The last one was in 2006.

John picked up a large, heavy book and threw it straight at me.

Jane Eyre

My name is Jane Eyre and my story begins when I was ten. I was living with my aunt, Mrs Reed, because my mother and father were both dead. Mrs Reed was rich. Her house was large and beautiful, but I was not happy there. Mrs Reed had three children, Eliza, John and Georgiana. My cousins were older than I. They never wanted to play with me and they were often unkind. I was afraid of them.

I was most afraid of my cousin John. He enjoyed frightening me and making me feel unhappy. One afternoon, I hid from him in a small room. I had a book with a lot of pictures in it and I felt quite happy. John and his sisters were with their mother.

But then John decided to look for me.

'Where's Jane Eyre?' he shouted, 'Jane! Jane! Come out!' He could not find me at first – he was not quick or clever. But then Eliza, who was clever, found my hiding place.

'Here she is!' she shouted. I had to come out. And John was waiting for me.

'What do you want?' I asked him.

'I want you to come here,' John said. I went and stood in front of him. He looked at me for a long time, and then suddenly he hit me. 'Now go and stand near the door!' he said.

I was very frightened. I knew that John wanted to hurt me. I went and stood near the door. Then John picked up a large, heavy book and threw it straight at me. The book hit me on the head and I fell.

'You cruel boy!' I shouted. 'You always want to hurt me. Look!' I touched my head. There was blood on it.

John became angrier. He ran across the room and started to hit me again and again. I was hurt and afraid, so I hit him back.

1

When at last I woke up, I was in my bed. The doctor was there.
'What happened?' I asked him.

Mrs Reed heard the noise and hurried into the room. She was very angry. She did not seem to notice the blood on my head.

'Jane Eyre! You bad girl!' she shouted. 'Why are you hitting your poor cousin? Take her away! Take her to the red room and lock the door!'

The red room was cold and dark. I was very frightened. Nobody ever went into the red room at night. I cried for help, but nobody came. 'Please help me!' I called, 'Don't leave me here!'

But nobody came to open the door. I cried for a long time, and then everything suddenly went black. I remember nothing after that.

When at last I woke up, I was in my bed. My head was hurting. The doctor was there. 'What happened?' I asked him.

'You are ill, Jane,' the doctor answered. 'Tell me, Jane. Are you unhappy here with your aunt and your cousins?'

'Yes, I am,' I answered. 'I'm very unhappy.'

'I see,' said the doctor. 'Would you like to go away to school?' he asked.

'Oh, yes, I think so,' I told him. The doctor looked at me again, and then he left the room. He talked to Mrs Reed for a long time. They decided to send me away to school.

So not long afterwards, I left my aunt's house to go to school. Mrs Reed and my cousins were pleased when I went away. I was not really sad to leave. 'Perhaps I'll be happy at school,' I thought. 'Perhaps I'll have some friends there.'

♦

One night in January, after a long journey, I arrived at Lowood School. It was dark and the weather was cold, windy and rainy.

The school was very large, but it was not warm and comfortable, like Mrs Reed's house. A teacher took me into a big room. It was full of girls. There were about eighty girls there. The youngest girls were nine, and the eldest were about twenty. They all wore ugly brown dresses.

It was supper time. There was water to drink, and a small piece of bread to eat. I was thirsty, and drank some water. I could not eat anything because I felt too tired and too excited. After supper, all the girls went upstairs to bed. The teacher took me into a very long room. All the girls slept in this room. Two girls had to sleep in each bed.

Early in the morning, I woke up. It was still dark outside and the room was very cold. The girls washed themselves in cold water and put on their brown dresses. Then everybody went downstairs and the early morning lessons began.

3

A teacher took me into a big room. It was full of girls. There were about eighty girls there.

At last, it was time for breakfast. I was now very hungry. We went into the dining-room with the teachers. There was a terrible smell of burning food. We were all hungry, but when we tasted the food we could not eat it. It tasted terrible. Feeling very hungry, we all left the dining-room.

At nine o'clock, lessons began again. I looked round at the other girls. They looked very strange in their ugly brown dresses. I did not like the teachers. They seemed to be unkind and unfriendly.

Then at twelve o'clock, the head teacher, Miss Temple, came in. She was very pretty and her face was kind. 'I want to speak to all the girls,' she said. 'I know that you could not eat your breakfast this morning,' she told us. 'So now you will have some bread and cheese and a cup of coffee.' The other teachers looked surprised. 'I'll pay for this meal,' Miss Temple said. The girls were very pleased.

After this meal, we went out into the garden. The girls' brown dresses were too thin for the cold winter weather. Most of the girls looked cold and unhappy, and some of them looked very ill. I walked around and looked at the girls and at the school and the garden. But I did not speak to anyone, and nobody spoke to me.

One of the girls was reading a book. 'Is your book interesting?' I asked her.

'I like it,' she answered.

'Does this school belong to Miss Temple?' I asked.

'No, it doesn't,' she answered. 'It belongs to Mr Brocklehurst. He buys all our food and all our clothes.'

The girl's name was Helen Burns. She was older than I was. I liked her immediately. She became my friend.

Helen told me that many of the girls were ill because they were always cold and hungry. Mr Brocklehurst was not a kind man. The clothes he bought for the girls were not warm enough for the winter, and there was never enough food to eat.

I went to Miss Temple's room. Helen Burns was lying there in a little bed. She was now very thin, and her face was white.

After a few months, many of the girls at Lowood School became seriously ill. Lessons stopped, and I and the other girls who were not ill spent all our time out in the fields near the school. The weather was now warm and sunny. It was a happy time for us, but my friend Helen Burns was not with us. She had to stay in bed. She was very ill.

One evening, I went to Miss Temple's room. Helen Burns was lying there in a little bed. She was now very thin, and her face was white. She spoke to me in a low voice. 'Jane,' she said, 'it's good to see you. I want to say goodbye to you.'

'Why?' I asked her. 'Are you going away?'

'Yes, I am,' Helen answered. 'I'm going far away.'

That night she died.

During that summer, many other girls in the school died too. Mr Brocklehurst sold the school, and it became a happier place.

I stayed at the school until I was eighteen and then I had to find a job. I wanted to become a teacher.

I wrote a letter to a newspaper. I said I was a young teacher, who wanted a job working in a family. Then I waited for an answer. At last, an answer came. It was from a lady, Mrs Fairfax, who lived at a place called Thornfield Hall. She needed a teacher for a little girl. So I packed my clothes in a small bag and travelled to Thornfield Hall.

♦

I felt very excited when I arrived at Thornfield Hall. The house was large, but it seemed very quiet. Mrs Fairfax met me at the door. She was an old lady with a kind face.

'Sit down, Miss Eyre,' she said. 'You look tired after your journey. Later, you will meet Adèle.'

'Is Adèle my student?' I asked.

'Yes, she is. She is French. Mr Rochester wants you to teach her English.'

'Who is Mr Rochester?' I asked.

Mrs Fairfax looked surprised. 'Did you not know? Thornfield Hall belongs to Mr Rochester,' she answered. 'I only work for him.'

'Is Mr Rochester here now?' I asked.

'No. He is away. He does not come very often to Thornfield. I do not know when he will return.'

Later, I met Adèle. She was a pretty little girl. I spoke to her in French, and began to teach her English. She enjoyed her lessons, and I enjoyed teaching her. I liked Adèle and I liked Mrs Fairfax, too. It was quiet at Thornfield Hall, and sometimes I felt a little bored, but everybody was kind to me there.

One afternoon, I walked to the village to post a letter. It was winter, and there was ice on the road. As I was walking back to Thornfield Hall, I heard a noise behind me. It was a horse. A man was riding towards Thornfield Hall. I stood on one side and the horse went past. The man did not see me. He was a stranger with dark hair. Suddenly, with a loud noise, the stranger's horse fell down on the ice. The man was lying on the ground, trying to get up. I ran forward to help.

'Are you hurt, sir?' I asked him.

The stranger looked surprised to see me. 'A little,' he answered. 'Could you help me to catch my horse? That's right. Now could you bring the horse here, please? Thank you.' The stranger tried to stand up, but his leg was hurting too much. He looked at me again. 'Could you help me to get up on its back again? Good. Thank you, Miss.'

I watched him as he rode away. 'Who is he?' I asked myself. 'He is not handsome, but he has an interesting face. I would like to know him.'

When I got back to Thornfield, everybody was very excited. Mrs Fairfax was very busy. 'What's happening?' I asked her.

'Oh, Miss Eyre,' said Mrs Fairfax, 'it is Mr Rochester! He has suddenly come back! But he will probably go away again soon. Now, Miss Eyre, you must go and put on your best dress. Mr Rochester wants to meet you and Adèle after dinner.'

Later that evening, I took Adèle to Mr Rochester's room. I felt rather afraid of meeting Mr Rochester. I went quietly into the room and saw a man there. I knew him. It was the man on the horse. So the interesting stranger was Mr Rochester!

Mr Rochester did not go away again. He was busy every day but sometimes in the evenings he talked to me. He was usually serious, and he did not smile or laugh very often, but he was

A man was riding towards Thornfield Hall. Suddenly, with a loud noise, the stranger's horse fell down on the ice.

Mr Rochester was asleep and the bed was on fire! Quickly, I took
some water and threw it all over the bed.

interesting and I was not afraid of him. I began to enjoy myself
more at Thornfield Hall.

♦

One night, I woke up suddenly. It was about two o'clock in the
morning. I thought I heard a sound. Everything was very quiet.
I listened carefully and the sound came again. Someone was
walking about outside my room.

'Who's there?' I called. Nobody answered. I felt cold and
frightened. The house was silent. I tried to sleep again.

Then I heard a laugh. It was a terrible, cruel laugh! I listened.
Someone was walking away, going up the stairs to the attic.
What was happening? I decided to go and find Mrs Fairfax. I put

on some clothes and left my room. The house was quiet now, but suddenly I could smell smoke. Something was burning! I ran to find out.

The smoke was coming from Mr Rochester's room. I ran into the room and looked around. Mr Rochester was asleep in his bed, and the bed was on fire! 'What can I do?' I thought. Quickly, I looked around the room. Luckily, there was some water in one corner. As quickly as I could, I took the water and threw it all over the bed. Mr Rochester woke up.

'What's happening?' he shouted. 'Jane! Is it you? What are you doing?'

'Mr Rochester,' I said, 'your bed is on fire! You must get up at once.'

He jumped out of bed. There was water everywhere and the fire was still smoking. 'Jane, you've saved me from the fire! How did you know about it? Why did you wake up?' Mr Rochester asked. I told him about the noise outside my door and the terrible laugh.

Mr Rochester looked serious and angry. 'I must go upstairs to the attic. Stay here and wait for me, please. Do not wake Mrs Fairfax.' He left the room and I waited for him.

At last, he came back. He was still looking very serious. 'You can go back to bed, now, Jane. Everything is all right now.'

'Who lives in the attic?' I asked Mrs Fairfax the next day.

'Only Grace Poole,' she answered. 'She is one of the servants. She is a strange woman.'

I remembered Grace Poole. She was a strange, silent woman, who did not often speak to the other servants. So perhaps it was Grace Poole who walked around the house late at night and laughed strangely outside the doors.

That evening, when Adèle finished her lessons, I went downstairs. Mrs Fairfax met me. 'Mr Rochester left the house early this morning,' she said. 'He is going to stay with his friends. I think he will stay with them for some weeks. I do not know when he will come back.'

For several weeks, the house was very quiet again. Mr Rochester stayed with his friends and I continued my lessons with Adèle. I did not hear the strange and terrible laugh at night again.

One day, Mrs Fairfax showed me a letter from Mr Rochester. 'He is coming back,' she said, 'and he is bringing a lot of visitors with him. I am going to be very busy getting everything ready. Miss Blanche Ingram is coming too. She is very beautiful.'

Mr Rochester and his friends arrived. The visitors were all rich, important people. Miss Blanche Ingram was among them. She was beautiful but very proud. Some of the visitors were nice to me, but the others did not notice me. I was too poor and unimportant. Miss Ingram never spoke to me. She was not interested in me, but she seemed to be interested in Mr Rochester. She always seemed to enjoy her conversations with him. They often went out riding together.

'I think Mr Rochester will marry Miss Ingram,' said Mrs Fairfax.

But was Mr Rochester interested in Blanche Ingram? He seemed to like her, but he did not look very happy when they were together.

◆

One evening, a new visitor came to Thornfield Hall. He was a quiet young man with dark hair called Mr Mason. He came to see Mr Rochester on business. Mr Mason told us that he and Mr Rochester were old friends, but Mr Rochester was not very pleased to see Mr Mason. When Mr Rochester heard the name 'Mr Mason, from the West Indies', he was surprised and his face turned white.

Blanche Ingram seemed to be interested in Mr Rochester. They often went out riding together.

That night, Mr Rochester and Mr Mason talked for a long time. At last, very late at night, they went to bed. Soon, everyone in the house was asleep. Suddenly, I woke up. I heard a terrible scream from somewhere over my head. Then everything was very quiet again. I listened carefully, and then I heard a lot of noise from above my head. There seemed to be fighting in the room above. Then there was another scream.

'Help! Help!' someone shouted. There was more fighting. Then a voice called out 'Rochester! Come quickly! Help me!'

A door opened, and I heard someone running up the stairs to the attic. I quickly put on some clothes and opened my door. Everybody in the house was awake now. The visitors were all standing outside their doors.

'What's happening? Is there a fire? What was that noise?' they asked.

Mr Rochester came down from the attic. 'Please don't worry,' he told his friends. 'Everything is all right.'

'But what's happening?' somebody asked.

'One of the servants had a bad dream and started to scream,' Mr Rochester said. 'But everything is all right now. Please go back to bed.'

Slowly, all Mr Rochester's visitors returned to their rooms. I too went back to my room, but I did not go back to bed. I sat and looked out of the window. The house was very quiet now. There were no sounds from the attic.

Then someone knocked on my door. I opened it. Mr Rochester stood outside. 'Jane, come with me please,' he told me, 'but come quietly . . . follow me.'

I followed Mr Rochester up to the attic. He unlocked the door of a room and we went inside.

'Wait here,' Mr Rochester told me. I stood next to the door.

There was another door on the opposite side of the room. From behind this door I could hear a terrible sound. It was like an angry animal. Mr Rochester left me and went through this door. Once again, I heard that terrible, cruel laugh! Was Grace Poole behind the door? Mr Rochester spoke to someone inside the room, and then came out and locked the door again.

'Come here, Jane,' he told me quietly. I came further into the room. There was a large bed in the room. Mr Mason was lying on the bed. His face was white and his eyes were closed. There was a lot of blood on his shirt. He did not move.

'Is he dead?' I asked.

'No,' answered Mr Rochester. 'He isn't badly hurt but I must go and bring the doctor for him. Will you stay with him until I get back?'

The man on the bed moved, and tried to speak. Mr Rochester turned to him. 'Don't try to talk, Mason. Jane, do not speak to him, please. There must be no conversation between you.'

Mr Rochester hurried out of the room. I waited for him with the silent man on the bed. I was frightened. I knew that Grace Poole was in the next room. For a long time, I waited for Mr Rochester to return. 'When will he come back?' I asked myself.

At last morning came and Mr Rochester returned with the doctor. While the doctor was looking after Mr Mason, Mr Rochester spoke to me. 'Thank you for all your help, Jane. Mason is going to leave Thornfield Hall now. The doctor will take him away,' he told me.

We helped Mr Mason down the stairs and out of the house. It was still early, and the other people in the house were still asleep.

'Take care of poor Mason,' said Mr Rochester to the doctor. 'Soon he will be able to go back home to the West Indies.'

Before he left, Mr Mason said something very strange. 'Look after her, Rochester,' he said. 'Promise to look after her.'

ESL CENTER

I waited for Mr Rochester's return with the silent man on the bed.
I was frightened, I knew that Grace Poole was in the next room.

Mr Rochester looked sad. 'I promise. I will always look after her.'

I started to go back to the house. 'Don't go, Jane,' said Mr Rochester. 'Come into the garden. Talk to me.'

We went into the garden. 'What a night!' he said. 'Were you frightened, Jane?'

'Yes, I was frightened. Up there, in the next room ... there was someone ... that terrible laugh ... Mr Rochester, will Grace Poole go away now?'

'No,' he replied. 'But don't worry about Grace Poole. Try to forget about her. She isn't dangerous. It is Mason I am worrying about.'

I was surprised to hear this. 'Mr Mason? But he is frightened. He can't hurt you.'

Mr Rochester looked sad. 'I know Mason does not want to hurt me, but he could say something that will hurt me. I shall be happier when he goes back to the West Indies.'

♦

Later that day, I got a surprising letter. Mrs Reed, my aunt, was dying and she wanted to see me. It was a long journey to her home. When I got there, I heard that my cousin John was dead. Mrs Reed was very ill. At first, she did not want to speak to me. Then one day, when I was sitting by her bed, she showed me a letter. It was from my uncle, my father's brother, who lived in Madeira. This was the letter:

> *Dear Mrs Reed,*
> *Please help me. I want to find my brother's daughter,*
> *Jane Eyre. I am a rich man and I have no children. I*
> *want Jane Eyre to come and live with me.*
>
> *Yours sincerely,*
> *John Eyre.*

I read the letter and looked at the date on it. 'But, Mrs Reed,' I said, 'this is an old letter. You got it three years ago!'

'I know,' she said, 'but I never liked you, Jane Eyre. After I read the letter, I wrote to your uncle. I told him you were dead. I told him you died at Lowood School. Now go away! Leave me!'

Soon afterwards, Mrs Reed died, and I returned to Thornfield Hall. It was summer, and the fields around Thornfield Hall were very quiet and beautiful. For me, it was the most beautiful place in the world. It was my home now.

'Adèle will be pleased to see me,' I thought. 'But what about Mr Rochester? He is the person I most want to see. But does he want to see me? Perhaps by now he is already married to Blanche Ingram. If they are not already married, they will be married very soon.' I felt sad when I thought about Mr Rochester and Blanche Ingram. 'So I must soon leave this beautiful place,' I thought. 'I can't stay here when Mr Rochester is married. I will never see Thornfield Hall again. And worse than that, I will never see Mr Rochester again.'

As I came near the house, I met Mr Rochester. When I saw that he looked pleased to see me, I felt happier. Adèle and Mrs Fairfax were happy to see me too. 'The visitors have all left now,' said Mrs Fairfax. It is very quiet here. It is good to see you again.'

'Yes, this is my home,' I thought. 'I've always been happy here. How can I leave it?'

I started to work, teaching Adèle again. Everything was the same as before. Mr Rochester still said nothing about getting married to Blanche Ingram. Then one evening, he saw me in the garden. 'Come and talk to me, Jane,' he said.

I went towards him. 'Now,' I thought, 'he's going to tell me that he is going to get married.'

'Are you happy here, Jane?' he asked.

'Yes, I am, very happy,' I answered.

'And you like Adèle and Mrs Fairfax?'

'Very much,' I said.

'You'll be sad to leave them,' he said.

I looked away. 'Now he is going to tell me that I must leave because he is going to be married,' I thought. I looked at him. 'Yes,' I answered, 'I will be very sad to leave.'

'But you must leave, you know,' Mr Rochester said.

'Must I? Must I leave soon?'

'Yes, soon.'

'Then you are going to get married.'

'Yes, I am going to get married. Adèle must go to school, and you must get a new job. I will find you one. Far from here.'

'Far from here?' I asked. 'But then I'll never see Thornfield Hall again, and . . . and I'll never see you again, Mr Rochester.'

'Oh, when you are far from here, you'll soon forget me,' he said.

'No,' I thought, 'you will forget me perhaps, but I will never forget you.'

'Never,' I answered him, at last. And I started to cry. I could not speak.

He watched me carefully, then at last he spoke again. 'Perhaps you do not need to go,' he said. 'Perhaps you can stay here when I am married?'

Did Mr Rochester think that I had no feelings? Did he not understand how I felt? Were my feelings so unimportant? I now felt angry.

'No,' I told him. 'I could never stay. I will not stay. Miss Ingram . . . Miss Ingram will be your wife. I know that I am not rich and beautiful like Miss Ingram. I am poor and unimportant.

Mr Rochester wanted to marry me! He wanted me to be his wife!

But I can still feel sadness. And if you marry Miss Ingram, I must leave here.'

Mr Rochester looked at me, and then he smiled. 'I don't want you to go, Jane. And I am not going to marry Miss Ingram. Don't get excited. I want you to stay here. It's you I want to marry.'

I could not believe him. 'Now you are laughing at me,' I said.

'No, I am not,' he answered. 'I want you to marry me, Jane. Will you marry me?'

He looked at me so seriously that at last I did believe him. Mr Rochester wanted to marry me! He wanted me to be his wife!

'Yes, I will marry you,' I answered.

'I will make you happy, Jane,' he said. 'No one will stop us,' he continued, with a strange, half-sad look. I could not understand that look, but I was too happy to be worried about it.

It grew dark. The wind began to blow, and it started to rain, so we walked together back to the house.

♦

My wedding day was only a month later. Two nights before the wedding, I was in bed, asleep. My wedding dress was in the room. It was a windy night. The wind made a strange sound. Suddenly, I woke up. There was a light in the room. I thought it was morning, but it was still dark outside.

Someone was in my room. Was it Mrs Fairfax? Was it Grace Poole? It was neither of them. It was a woman, but I did not know her. She was a big woman, tall and strong. Her black hair was long and thick. Her clothes were long and white. At first I did not see her face. She took my dress and held it in front of her. She looked at herself in the mirror. Then I saw her face!

It was the most terrible face! The woman's eyes were large and red and her face was purple. She looked angry, cruel and frightening.

Then she took my dress, and angrily tore it to pieces. She threw the pieces of the dress on the floor. Next, she went to the window, and looked out. Then she started to come towards my bed. I was so frightened that I could not move. I could not scream for help. I lay still in bed. 'Is she going to kill me?' I thought. But suddenly the light disappeared and the room went dark.

When I woke up, it was morning. The sun was shining. At once, I remembered that strange and frightening woman. Did it all really happen or was it a dream? Did she really come into my room in the middle of the night? Then I saw my wedding dress.

'Jane, I think you had a bad dream, I think it was perhaps Grace Poole who really tore your dress.'

It was lying on the floor, torn to pieces, I picked up the pieces of the dress. So it was all true! That terrible woman was real!

When I told Mr Rochester about the woman and showed him my dress, he looked very worried and was silent for a long time.

'Jane, I think you had a bad dream,' he said at last. 'I think it was perhaps Grace Poole who really tore your dress, but in your dream it was some stranger.'

I was not sure about this, but I said nothing. That night, the night before the wedding, I slept in Adèle's room.

My wedding day came, and we went to the church. But

22

the wedding did not happen. In the church, while the clergyman was speaking, someone threw open the doors at the back and shouted 'Stop the wedding! Mr Rochester cannot get married! He has got a wife already! He is married to my sister!'

Everybody in the church turned round to see the speaker. It was Mr Mason, the man from the West Indies. But who was his sister? How could Mr Rochester be married? I could not believe it. My heart turned to ice. I looked at Mr Rochester. His face was white and hard. But he did not say that Mr Mason was mistaken.

'But where is Mr Rochester's wife, your sister?' the clergyman asked Mr Mason. 'Where does she live?'

'She lives at Thornfield Hall,' answered Mr Mason. 'She is still alive. I saw her there last April.'

'At Thornfield Hall!' the clergyman said. 'But I know of no Mrs Rochester at Thornfield Hall. There must be some mistake.'

Mr Rochester was silent for a long time. 'I can explain,' he said at last. 'I'll tell you everything. It is true. My wife is living at Thornfield Hall. We got married fifteen years ago in the West Indies, when I was a young man. My wife's name was Bertha Mason. She is Mason's sister. Soon after the wedding, Bertha became very strange. Slowly, she became mad and dangerous. She wanted to kill me, and she tried to kill anybody who came near her. Last April, she tried to kill her brother, Mr Mason.'

'Nobody knows about Bertha, nobody knows that she is my wife. This young lady, Jane Eyre, knows nothing about her. A nurse, Grace Poole, looks after Bertha.' Mr Rochester's face was dark and serious. 'Come with me,' he said, 'now I will take you all to see her.'

We all left the church. Without speaking, we returned to Thornfield Hall. When we got there, Mr Rochester took us up to the attic. He took out a key and unlocked the door. Grace Poole was there, and in the room with her there was a

Someone threw open the doors at the back of the church, and shouted 'Stop the wedding!'

frightening woman, the terrible woman that I saw in my bedroom, the person with the cruel, mad laugh! She was the person who tried to kill Mr Mason and who set fire to Mr Rochester's room! She was mad. But she was Mr Rochester's wife and I could not marry him.

Poor Mr Rochester! I felt sorry for him. But I could not now stay at Thornfield Hall.

'I must leave my home for ever,' I thought, with a heavy heart. 'I can never come back and I will never see Mr Rochester again.'

Sadly, I put a few ordinary clothes into a small bag. I did not take my beautiful new clothes. I took a little money and quietly left Thornfield Hall early one morning. I did not say goodbye to anybody and nobody saw me leave.

♦

I wanted to travel as far away from Thornfield Hall as I could. I spent all my money. I travelled for two days and nights until at last I arrived at a place where there were no towns or villages and very few houses. I had no money now to buy food. I was very tired and very hungry.

It was evening and it was getting dark. I could see only one house. I went to the house and looked through the window. There were two young women in the room. They looked kind, so I knocked on the door. A servant opened it.

'Who are you?' she asked. 'What do you want?'

'I'm a stranger,' I said. 'I haven't any money or food. I'm tired and hungry. Please help me.'

The servant looked at me for a long time. 'I'll give you some bread,' she answered at last. 'But then you must go away.' She left me and came back with a piece of bread. 'Now go!' she said. 'You can't stay here.'

But I was too tired to move. I sat down on the ground by the door. 'Nobody will help me,' I said. 'I will die.'

I did not know, but someone was listening and watching me.
'You won't die' he said.

I did not know, but someone was listening and watching me.

'You won't die,' he said, 'Who are you?' I looked up and saw a tall young man. He knocked loudly on the door. The servant opened it again.

'Hannah,' the man asked, 'who is this young woman?'

'I don't know,' said the servant, Hannah. 'I told her to go away, but she's still here. Go away!' she said to me.

'No, Hannah, she can't go away. She is ill and she needs our help. She must come inside,' the man said.

They took me into the house. The room was warm. The two young women came to talk to me.

'What's your name?' they asked.

'My name's Jane Elliot,' I said. I did not want anyone to know my real name. I did not want Mr Rochester to find me. I wanted to start again.

My new friends gave me some food and took me to a bedroom where I slept for a long time.

After a few days I felt better, and was able to talk to my kind new friends. Their names were Diana and Mary Rivers. The man was their brother. His name was St John Rivers and he was a clergyman. St John was a very handsome young man with fair hair and blue eyes. He was always very serious. He did not often laugh or smile. He was planning to go to India to work.

His sisters were more friendly but I did not want to tell them about Mr Rochester. I thanked them for their kindness. 'I have no family,' I said. 'My parents are both dead. I was at Lowood School for six years. After that, I got a job with a family, but I had to leave suddenly. I didn't do anything wrong. Please believe me.

'Don't talk now,' said Diana. 'You are tired.'

'You will want a new job now,' said St John.

'Yes,' I replied. 'As soon as possible.'

'Good. I will help you.'

A month later, Diana and Mary left their home to work as teachers in the south of England. St John asked me to teach the children who lived near his church. They were poor children and the school was very small. I was the only teacher.

I enjoyed my work. I did not have much money and I had to work very hard. I lived in a very small house near the school. There were not many people there, but St John was very kind and gave me books to read. In my free time, I read and painted pictures. Sometimes, St John visited me in the evenings.

One evening, he came to my house when I was just finishing a painting. He looked at some of my pictures. Then he looked again, more closely, at one of the paintings. Without saying anything, he tore a piece of paper off the bottom of the painting, and put it carefully into his pocket. Then, quite suddenly, he left. I was very surprised. What a strange person he was!

The next day it snowed. I thought no visitors would come that day. But in the evening there was a knock on the door. It was St John. He was wet and cold.

'Why have you come? Is there bad news?' I asked. 'Are your sisters all right?'

'Don't worry. There is no bad news. Diana and Mary are both well,' he answered. He sat down in front of the fire. I waited but he said nothing. 'How strange he is!' I thought. 'Why did he come here when the weather is so bad? Perhaps he is bored. His sisters are far away.'

St John sat and thought for a long time. At last, he spoke.

'I know your story,' St John said. 'I know about your parents, and about Mrs Reed. I know about Lowood School. And I know about Thornfield Hall and about Mr Rochester. I also know about Mr Rochester's wife. So now I know why you came here without any money. I know why you left Thornfield Hall. Mr Rochester must be a very bad man.'

'Oh, no. He isn't,' I said.

'I have had a letter,' said St John, 'from a man in London called Mr Briggs. He wants to find you. He asked about Jane Eyre. You call yourself Jane Elliot, but I know your real name is Jane Eyre. Look!' St John showed me a piece of paper. It was the piece of paper from the bottom of my painting. My real name, Jane Eyre, was on it.

'Did Mr Briggs say anything about Mr Rochester?' I asked. 'How is Mr Rochester?' I only wanted to know about Mr Rochester. I still loved him.

'Mr Briggs doesn't know anything about your Mr Rochester,' said St John. 'He wrote to me about your uncle, Mr Eyre of Madeira. Your uncle is dead. He has left you all his money. You are a very rich young woman.'

For a long time, I was too surprised to speak. I was rich now, but I was not excited. I tried to understand what it meant to be rich.

'I can't understand,' I said at last. 'Why did Mr Briggs write to you?'

'Because,' St John said, 'Mr Eyre of Madeira was also our uncle. He was my mother's brother. When he died, he left all his money to you, Jane Eyre.'

'Then you, Diana and Mary are my cousins!' I said. 'This is wonderful news! Our uncle's money is for all of us. Diana and Mary can come home, and we can all live together.' It was good to have money, but it was even better to have three cousins.

So, just before Christmas, Diana and Mary came home. I worked hard to make their old house comfortable. 'Diana and Mary will like it,' I thought. 'But what about St John? He's a strange man. He's like stone, hard and cold. He's pleased to see his sisters, but still he does not really look happy.'

Diana, Mary and I began to live quietly and comfortably together. St John still wanted to go to India. I was happy living with my cousins but I still thought about Mr Rochester every day. Where was he? Was he happy? I wrote to the lawyer, Mr Briggs, but Mr Briggs knew nothing about Mr Rochester. Then I wrote to Mrs Fairfax at Thornfield Hall. I waited for a letter from her, but no letter came. I wrote to Mrs Fairfax again; perhaps she did not get my first letter. Again there was no answer. At last, a letter did come for me, but it was only a letter from Mr Briggs about my uncle's money. I began to cry.

While I was crying, St John came into the room and saw me. 'Jane,' he said, 'come for a walk with me. No, don't call Diana and Mary. I want to talk to you.'

We walked along the side of the river. At first, St John said nothing. At last, he turned to me. 'Jane, I'm going to India in six weeks and I want you to come with me.'

I was surprised. Why did St John want me to go to India with him? How could I help him? I was not strong and serious like him.

'As your helper?' I asked. 'I don't think . . .'

'No, not as my helper. As my wife. I want to marry you, so that we can work together in India. There are many poor people there. They need our help.'

Now I was even more surprised. I felt sure that St John did not love me. And I did not want to marry him. I could not marry him. I still loved Mr Rochester.

'But I can't go to India,' I said. 'I don't know how to help the people there. I'm not like you.'

St John looked at me seriously. 'Oh, that doesn't matter. I'll tell you what to do and you'll quickly learn. You always worked hard in the village school. You'll work hard in India, too.'

I thought for a long time. St John, my cousin, needed my help. He was going to do very useful work in India. At last, I continued. 'Perhaps I can help you, but I must be free. I cannot marry you. You're like my brother,' I said.

St John looked at me. His handsome face was cold and serious,

I said 'Perhaps I can help you but I must be free. I cannot marry you. You're like my brother.'

like stone. 'That's not possible. You must be my wife. I don't want a sister. I don't want you to marry another man. I want you to stay with me, to work with me, until we die.'

I felt cold and sad. I remembered my love for Mr Rochester and the way he always spoke to me. St John was different. He wanted me to marry him, but I knew he did not love me. I wanted to help him, but not to marry him. He was a good man, but I did not love him. I did not know what to say to him.

'I'm going away for two weeks,' St John continued. 'When I come back, I want your answer. I hope you will decide to marry me. You can't just stay here doing nothing.'

When I went back into the house, Diana spoke to me. 'Jane, you look unhappy. Your face is white. What is happening?'

I told her. 'St John asked me to marry him.'

'But that's wonderful!' she said. 'Now he will stay in England. He won't go to India. He'll stay here with us.'

'No,' I said, 'He wants me to go to India with him.'

'But you cannot go to India!' she said. 'You aren't strong enough.'

'I won't go,' I told her, 'because I can't marry St John. And now I'm afraid he's angry with me. He's a good man, but he doesn't understand how ordinary people feel.'

'I know,' Diana said. 'Our brother is a very good man, but he sometimes seems cold and hard.'

That night, I thought about St John for a long time. I did not know what to do. I did not love him, and he did not love me. But perhaps I could help him in India. I did not know what to do. The night was very quiet.

Suddenly, I thought I heard a voice. 'Jane! Jane! Jane!' it called. It was Mr Rochester's voice.

'Where are you?' I cried. But there was no answer. There was no one there. Was it only a dream? No, I knew that somewhere, far away, Mr Rochester needed me. 'I must go and find him,' I thought.

♦

The next day, I went to look for Mr Rochester. After a long journey, I arrived at Thornfield Hall. I walked for the last two miles to the house. I was excited; I was hurrying to see my old home again. The trees were the same, the road was the same. I arrived at the house and stopped . . . and stood and looked.

It was terrible! Where was Thornfield Hall, my beautiful home? No one could live here now. Now I understood why Mrs Fairfax never answered my letters. The walls of the house were still standing, but the windows were empty and dark and there was no roof. The grass was long and there were no flowers in the

I arrived at the house and stopped . . . and stood and looked.
It was terrible! No one could live here now.

garden. The broken walls of the Hall were black and silent. The only sounds were the birds and the wind. Where was Mrs Fairfax now? Where was little Adèle? And where was Mr Rochester?

I hurried back to the village to find out. I asked a man in the village to tell me about Thornfield Hall.

'No one lives there now,' he told me. 'Last autumn, Thornfield Hall burned down. It was terrible. The house burned down in the middle of the night.'

'How did it happen?' I asked him.

'They think Mr Rochester's wife started it. Nobody ever saw her, but people say she was mad. People think she started a fire in her room in the attic. When it happened, the house was almost empty. Mr Rochester was in the house, but the little girl, Adèle, was away at school and old Mrs Fairfax was staying with some friends, many miles away. It seems that Mr Rochester did not want to see anybody at that time. People say he seemed very unhappy. They say that he wanted to marry a young woman, but she ran away.'

'Tell me about the fire,' I said.

'When the fire started,' he continued, 'Mr Rochester got all the servants out of the house, then he went back in to save his wife. She was still in the attic. But she climbed up on to the roof. I saw her there. She stood on the roof, shouting and waving her arms. Mr Rochester tried to help her, but he could do nothing. Suddenly, she fell from the roof.'

'Did she die?' I asked.

'Yes, she did. She died immediately, and Mr Rochester was very badly hurt. He could not get out of the burning house in time. When at last he came out, he was blind, and he had lost one hand.' The man shook his head.

So Mr Rochester was still alive! He was hurt, but he was not dead. Suddenly, I began to hope again. I continued to question the man.

'Where does Mr Rochester live now?' I asked. 'Does he live in England?'

'Yes,' the man answered. 'He cannot travel far, poor man. He lives at Ferndean, about thirty miles from here. It is a quiet place. He lives there quietly with two servants. He never has any visitors.'

I decided to go to Ferndean at once. I arrived there just before dark. As I got near the house, the front door opened and a man came out. I knew at once it was Mr Rochester. But he was very different now. He was still tall and strong, and his hair was still black. But his face looked sad, and he could not walk without help. At last, he turned and went sadly back into the house.

The servant, Mary, who answered the door, knew me at once. She was very surprised to see me. I told her that I knew all about Mr Rochester and the fire at Thornfield Hall. 'Tell Mr Rochester that he has a visitor. But don't tell him who it is.'

'He won't see you, Miss Jane,' she said. 'He won't see anybody now.'

I went into the room.

'Who's there?' Mr Rochester asked. 'Is that you, Mary? Answer me! What's happening?'

'Will you have some water?' I asked him.

'Who's that? Tell me!' he said. He was surprised and excited.

'Mary knows me,' I said. 'I only came this evening.' I took his hand.

'Jane? Is it Jane?' he asked. 'Jane, is it really you?'

'Yes, it is,' I said. 'I'm so happy to be with you again. I'll never leave you now.'

'But Jane, where did you go? What happened to you? Why did you leave Thornfield Hall so suddenly? Why did you go away without any money? Why did you not stay and let me help you?' he asked.

'You know why I left,' I said. 'I am sorry you were worried.

But things are different now. I'm a rich woman,' I said. 'And I've got three cousins.' I told Mr Rochester all about my cousins and my new home.

'You do not need me now,' he said. 'But will you really stay with me?' There was hope in his voice again.

'Of course I will,' I said.

'But you're young. You'll want to get married some time. But not to me. I'm blind now and I can't do anything. You won't want to marry me. You'll want to marry some young man. What is your cousin, St John Rivers, like?' he asked. 'Is he an old man?'

'No. He is young and handsome.'

'Do you like him?' Mr Rochester asked.

'Yes, I do,' I answered. 'He's a very good man.'

'And does he like you?'

'Yes, I think so. He wants me to marry him.'

'And will you marry him?'

'No. I will not marry him. I do not love him.'

Mr Rochester looked suddenly happier. He took my hand. He was silent for a long time, and then he spoke. 'Jane, I can ask you again now: will you marry me?' he asked.

'Yes, I will,' I told him. At last, I felt really happy. And Mr Rochester, too, was no longer sad.

Three days later, I became Mr Rochester's wife.

I wrote to Diana and Mary. The news made them very happy. I also wrote to St John, but I had no answer from him. He went to India and continued to work very hard there. He never got married.

Mr Rochester and I are very happy together. We have been married for ten years now. Two years after we were married, Mr Rochester began to see again with one eye. He will never be able to see well, but he now can see me and he can see our children. Our story was a strange and sad one, and terrible things happened to us, but now at last we are happy together.

Then Mr Rochester spoke. 'Jane, I can ask you again now,' he said.
'Will you marry me?'

ACTIVITIES

Pages 1–7

Before you read

1 Look at the Word List at the back of this book. Check the words in your dictionary and answer these questions.

    a Which four words are people?

    b Which four words can describe people?

2 Read the Introduction to the book and answer these questions.

    a What do you know about Charlotte Brontë's mother and father?

    b Who were Currer, Ellis and Acton Bell? What did they do?

3 Look at the pictures on these pages. What do you think will happen to Jane? Do you think she has a happy life? Why (not)?

While you read

4 Write the name of the person from the story. Who:

    a is Jane's rich aunt? ....

    b is Jane's cruel cousin? ....

    c suggests that Jane should go away to school? ....

    d is the kind headteacher at Lowood School? ....

    e owns Lowood School? ....

    f is Jane's friend at school? ....

    g answers Jane's letter? ....

After you read

5 Discuss these questions.

    a Why is Jane unhappy with her aunt and cousins?

    b Is life better or worse for Jane at Lowood? Why?

    c Why does Jane leave the School and go to Thornfield Hall?

6 Talk with another student and compare these people.

    a Mrs Reed and Mr Brocklehurst

    b John Reed and Helen Burns

Pages 7–12

7 Look at the pictures and answer these questions.

    a Page 9: What is happening? What do you think Jane will do?

    b Page 10: What is she doing? Why?

8 In what ways will life at Thornfield Hall be better or worse for Jane than at Lowood School, do you think?

While you read

9 Are these sentences right (✓) or wrong (✗)?

    a Jane is going to teach English to Adèle, a French girl who lives in Mr Rochester's house.   .....

    b Jane is unhappy because Thornfield Hall is quiet and boring.   .....

    c After Jane helps the stranger to his feet, she wants to know him.   .....

    d When Jane hears a terrible, cruel laugh outside her bedroom door, she goes out of her room and up to the attic.   .....

    e Jane discovers a fire in Mr Rochester's bedroom and wakes him up.   .....

    f The servant Grace Poole is a strange woman who lives in the attic.   .....

    g After Mr Rochester goes to stay with friends, Jane hears the strange, cruel laugh at night again.   .....

    h Blanche Ingram is one of Mr Rochester's rich, important visitors and she is nice to Jane.   .....

After you read

10 Work with another student and have this conversation.

    Student A: You are Jane Eyre. It is the day after the fire. You want to know about the person who lives in the attic. You want to know who walks around the house at night and why.

    Student B: You are Mrs Fairfax. Answer Jane's questions. Tell her your opinion of Grace Poole and Mr Rochester.

11 How do these people feel?

    a Jane about Mr Rochester's visitors?

    b Mr Rochester about Blanche Ingram?

    c Mr Rochester about Jane?

Pages 12–21

Before you read

12 Who do you think set fire to Mr Rochester's bed? Why?

13 Look at the picture on page 16. In which room do you think Jane is? What is happening?

While you read

14 Finish sentences a–e. Write f–j.

    a Mr Rochester's surprised face went white when …   .....

    b Mr Rochester ran up the stairs because …   .....

    c Jane followed Mr Rochester to the attic where …   .....

    d Mr Rochester tells Jane that …   .....

    e As Mr Mason left with the doctor the next morning, …   .....

    f Mr Mason arrived from the West Indies.

    g she found Mr Mason lying on the bed with blood on his shirt.

    h Grace Poole is not dangerous.

    i someone in the attic was screaming.

    j he asked Mr Rochester to look after someone, a woman.

15 Circle the correct word in *italics*.

    a Jane's cruel cousin, John, is now *ill/dead*.

    b Three years earlier, Mrs Reed had a letter from Jane's *rich/poor* uncle. He wanted Jane to live with him in Madeira.

    c When Jane returns to Thornfield Hall, Mr Rochester *is/is not* already married to Blanche Ingram.

    d Jane *can't/must* leave if Mr Rochester marries Blanche Ingram.

    e Jane does not accept Mr Rochester's offer of marriage *at once/finally* because she can not believe him.

After you read

16 Discuss with another student: what is rather strange about Mr Rochester's:
  a 'friend' Mr Mason
  b order for silence between Jane and Mason
  c promise to Mason
  d worries about Mason

17 Who says or writes these sentences to who? And why?
  a 'I am a rich man and I have no children.'
  b 'I told him that you died at Lowood School.'
  c 'But you must leave, you know.'
  d 'I am poor and unimportant.'
  e 'No one will stop us.'

Pages 21–25

Before you read

18 Look at the pictures on pages 22 and 24. Do you think that Jane and Mr Rochester will have a happy wedding? Why (not)?

19 Give your opinion of these people. Will they be important to Jane and Mr Rochester's future? How?
  a Mr Mason
  b Grace Poole
  c John Eyre
  d Blanche Ingram

While you read

20 Put these in the correct order. Write 1–6.
  a ..... Jane learns that Mr Rochester's wife is mad and dangerous.
  b ..... Mr Rochester tells Jane that perhaps Grace Poole tore her dress.
  c ..... In the attic in Thornfield Hall, Mr Rochester shows Jane his mad wife, who tore Jane's wedding dress to pieces.
  d ..... Jane leaves Thornfield Hall without a word to anyone, taking only her ordinary clothes and a little money.

e ..... An angry stranger goes into Jane's room two nights before her wedding and tears Jane's wedding dress to pieces.

f ..... Mr Mason stops the wedding. He explains that Mr Rochester is married to his sister.

After you read

21 Why are these important in the story?

    a Jane's wedding dress

    b the West Indies

    c Mr Rochester's secret

22 Discuss these questions.

    a What are Mr Rochester's reasons for his marriage to Bertha?

    b What are his reasons for wanting to marry Jane?

    c Who do you think has suffered most?

    d Who has brought the greatest unhappiness to people in their lives?

Pages 25–32

Before you read

23 Jane has left Thornfield Hall with only a few clothes and a little money. Where do you think she will go? How will she live?

24 Look at the pictures on pages 26 and 31. What does the man in the pictures want, do you think?

While you read

25 Circle the best answer to each question.

    a Why did Jane tell the two young women that her name was Jane Elliot?

       • She didn't remember her name.

       • She didn't want Mr Rochester to find her.

       • She didn't like these people.

    b Where did the clergyman, St John Rivers want to go?

       • The south of England

       • America

       • India

c After Diana and Mary left, what did Jane enjoy doing?
- Working as a teacher
- Cleaning the house
- Painting the house

d St John discovers Jane's name and her life story. What other thing does he discover?
- That Mr Rochester is dead
- That Jane is his rich cousin
- That Jane's uncle is coming from Madeira

e Mr Briggs, the lawyer, wrote to St John about Jane's uncle, John Eyre. How did John Eyre know St John?
- He was St John's uncle.
- He was St John's boss.
- He was St John's cousin.

f Why can't Jane marry St John?
- She loves Mr Rochester
- She does not like India
- She is very rich

After you read

26 How do these things change Jane's life?
- **a** Jane's real name on her painting
- **b** Mr Briggs's letter to St John

27 What does Jane think is important in a marriage? How do you know?

Pages 32–36

Before you read

28 Jane says, 'I must go and find him.' Where will she go? What do you think she will find there? Why?

29 Look at the pictures on pages 33–37. Answer these questions.
- **a** What has happened to Thornfield Hall?
- **b** How does Jane feel about it, do you think?
- **c** Does she find Mr Rochester?
- **d** What do you think will happen with Mr Rochester?

While you read

30 Finish the sentences.

  a Jane discovers why Mrs Fairfax never answered her
....

  b A man in the village tells Jane that Thornfield Hall
....

  c Mr Rochester's wife died when she fell from the
....

  d In the fire, Mr Rochester lost one hand and he became
....

  e After three days at Ferndean, Jane becomes Mr Rochester's
....

After you read

31 How do you think Mr Rochester feels when:

  a the fire starts in Thornfield Hall?

  b his wife Bertha dies?

  c he loses his hand and becomes blind?

  d he hears Jane's voice?

  e he hears about St John Rivers from Jane?

  f he begins to see again with one eye?

32 Compare St John Rivers and Mr Rochester. Does Jane marry the right man, do you think? Why (not)?

Writing

33 Jane's life with her aunt and her cousins is very unhappy. Imagine you are Jane after her first week at Lowood School. Write in her private notebook about her new life at the school.

34 Write a newspaper report about the deaths of the girls at Lowood School. Write about Mr Brocklehurst and Miss Temple in your report.

35 Imagine you are Jane. You have sat up all night with Mr Mason and now it is the next morning. You do not understand Mr Rochester's fear of Mason. Write a description of your feelings for Mr Rochester and your opinion of him in your private notebook.

36 Imagine you are Mr Rochester. You have decided not to marry Blanche Ingram. Write a letter to her and explain why. Tell her about Jane and about the life that you want with her.

37 Write the conversation that Jane and Mr Rochester had the morning after the terrible woman tore Jane's wedding dress to pieces. What does Jane ask Mr Rochester, do you think? And what does he tell Jane?

38 You are Mr Rochester. Write his letter to Mr Mason after Bertha dies in the fire at Thornfield Hall. Tell him how his sister died. Tell him about the fire and about your life now.

39 Write Mr Briggs's letter to St John Rivers about John Eyre's death in Madeira.

40 Imagine you are St John Rivers. You are in India and you know from your sisters about Jane's marriage to Mr Rochester. Write a letter to Jane.

41 Which person in the story is the unkindest to Jane? How? Why? Write your answer.

42 Do you like this book? Why (not)? Write your answer.

WORD LIST

among (prep) in a group of

at once (adv) immediately

attic (n) the area under the roof of a house

blind (adj) not able to see

blow (v) to move the air; the wind *blows*; the past form is **blew**

take care of (v) to look after or do what is necessary

clergyman (n) a church man

cruel (adj) wanting to make people feel pain or sadness

eldest (adj) oldest (brother/sister or son/daughter)

forward (adv) towards a place that is in front

lawyer (n) somebody who has studied Law and uses it in his/her job

mad (adj) ill in the mind

no one (pron) nobody

pack (v) to put things into a box or bag before taking them
somewhere

rather (adv) quite or a little

servant (n) somebody who works for a person or family in their home

set fire to (v) to start burning something

several (quant) more than a few

stranger (n) somebody who you do not know

Yours sincerely   a polite ending in a business letter

Sense and Sensibility
Jane Austen

Elinor and Marianne Dashwood are two very different sisters. Marianne loves excitement and always shows her feelings; Elinor is quiet and has more good sense. They both fall in love and both suffer broken hearts. Will they ever find the right man to love and marry?

Vanity Fair
William Thackeray

Becky Sharp, an intelligent young lady with no family or money, becomes a governess. But this type of life is not enough for her. She has big plans for herself. Is she clever enough to find success? Will she marry and be happy? Or will life be unkind to her?

The Turn of the Screw
Henry James

A young woman comes to a big house to teach two young children. It's her first job and she wants to do it well. But she begins to see strange things – the ghosts of dead people. Do the ghosts want the children?

There are hundreds of Penguin Readers to choose from – world classics, film adaptations, modern-day crime and adventure, short stories, biographies, American classics, non-fiction, plays ...

For a complete list of all Penguin Readers titles, please contact your local Pearson Longman office or visit our website.